TEEN TITANS

Robin's C...

By Lisa Ryan-Herndon

Scholastic Inc.
New York   Toronto   London   Auckland   Sydney
Mexico City   New Delhi   Hong Kong   Buenos Aires

Many thanks to: Geno DuBois, Marlene Fenton, Chris Hooten, Glen Murakami and A.J. Vargas.

No part of this work may be reproduced in whole or in part, or stored in a retrieval system, or transmitted in any form or by any means, electronic, mechanical, photocopying, recording, or otherwise, without written permission of the publisher. For information regarding permission, write to Scholastic Inc., Attention: Permissions Department, 557 Broadway, New York, NY 10012.

ISBN: 0-439-63619-1

Published by Scholastic Inc.

SCHOLASTIC and associated logos are trademarks and/or registered trademarks of Scholastic Inc.

12 11 10 9 8 7 6 5 4 3 2 1   4 5 6 7 8/0

Pages 4-5, 6-7, 8-9, 15, 18-19, 24-25, 39, 29, 33, 34, 44-45, 48 ,51, 54-55, illustrated by Funnypages Productions.

Pages 11, 12,16, 21, 22, 42 (puppets), illustrated by Kevin Mackenzie.

Printed in the U.S.A.
First printing, August 2004

ROBIN'S CASE FILE

I wish I could ask for your help, team. I'd talk out strategies with Cyborg, laugh off my problems with Beast Boy, and believe like Starfire does that truth, justice, and the Teen Titans will be victorious in the end. But the team can't help me. Not this time. Not after what went down. Raven's right. I need to be alone if I'm going to crack this case.

I'm Robin, leader of the Teen Titans. We're proud of our high score at kicking bad-guy butt . . . except against Slade. We can't seem to take this guy down. Cyborg, Beast Boy, Raven, and Starfire are my teammates. They're also my friends. I care about them, a lot.

TEEN TITANS

WHO IS SLADE?

TITANS TEEN SLADE

I won't let them get hurt, even if it means I have to shut them out to keep them safe. I have to figure out what Slade's up to!

Slade's been calling the shots — always one step ahead of me — but not anymore.

I've been picking up the pieces to this puzzle all year long. Now I've got to put them together. I can do this. The World's Greatest Detective was my teacher, and there isn't a riddle he can't solve or a criminal he can't catch. I won't let him down — or my team. Everybody's counting on me to come up with the answers.

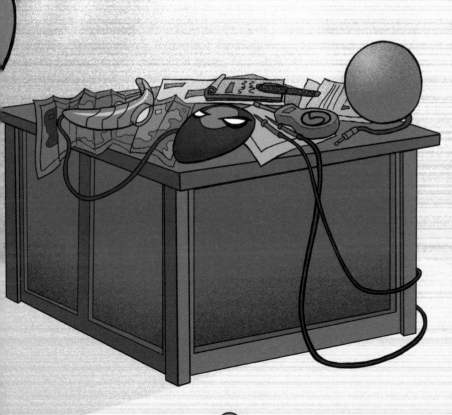

The day I first heard Slade's name was an ordinary day. We were hanging out at Titan Tower, our T-shaped, ten-story command center located on an island right off the city's coastline.

We had time before our regular training session, but Cy and BB lost the TV remote control again, and none of us would eat the furry blue stuff in the fridge or wash the dishes. So we went out for pizza. That's when everything changed.

They were only three — a girl, a boy, and a giant — against the five of us. Yet "The H.I.V.E." worked as a team and kicked our butts. Distract then divide, the oldest strategy in the book. Their victory was a hard lesson for us to learn: The Teen Titans are not invincible. We can lose, especially when we don't work together.

The H.I.V.E. was the perfect fighting force: well-organized, highly trained, and combat-equipped—everything the Titans were supposed to be. Who hired them to go after us, and why?

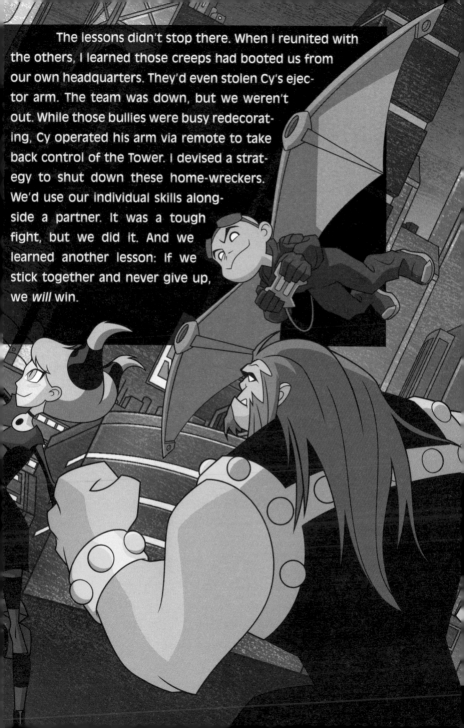

The lessons didn't stop there. When I reunited with the others, I learned those creeps had booted us from our own headquarters. They'd even stolen Cy's ejector arm. The team was down, but we weren't out. While those bullies were busy redecorating, Cy operated his arm via remote to take back control of the Tower. I devised a strategy to shut down these home-wreckers. We'd use our individual skills alongside a partner. It was a tough fight, but we did it. And we learned another lesson: If we stick together and never give up, we *will* win.

Jinx

Gizmo

THE H.I.V.E.

This mission qualified as the first entry in my case file. After it was all over, I did some digging on The H.I.V.E. The top students at The H.I.V.E. Academy for Extraordinary Young People could be hired by anyone to do any job, for the right price. They were hired to deliver a message; we sent back our own, loud and clear.

The girl's code name is Jinx. A gymnastic witch, she casts "bad luck" hexes using powerful, disruptive energy waves. Guaranteed if something was working fine, it'll break down the second she cartwheels into sight. This annoying girl demonstrated serious lack of good judgment by using my Utility Belt as a fashion statement and borrowing Raven's cloak. Once Beast Boy became a monkey on her back, she experienced her own bad luck.

The boy's code name is Gizmo. A mechanical genius, this kid's backpack houses more gear than Cy. He's got mechanical

Mammoth

wings, missiles, machine guns, electronic disruptors, holographic projectors, and a com unit keyed in to his mysterious boss. He likes order and trash-talking — he alphabetized Beast Boy's music while insulting his choices. This particular "kludge head" really enjoyed crashing his system with my own electronic disruptor disk.

The giant's code name is Mammoth. A genetically enhanced giant, his slamming fists and shockwave jumps are his favorite language. Alone, Cyborg couldn't take down Mammoth; however, the whole team did just fine. The saying is true: The bigger they are, the harder they fall. And Mammoth fell hard after Beast Boy's T rex gave him a smile. Serves him right for changing our T-shaped tower into an H-shaped block.

Electricity searches for the fastest way to get back into the ground. A conductor helps the flow of electricity. Water and metals are fast conductors. An insulator resists the flow of electricity. Glass, plastic, and rubber are strong insulators.

Cyborg's Walking Tour

Cyborg needs a helping hand to sneak from one end of Titan Tower to the other. His ejector arm must reach the main control panel located in the front room. Beware the unwelcome guests lurking around the next corner. And never, ever, go into Raven's room.

Opposite Reaction

Watch out! Jinx cast another "bad luck" hex. Her spell makes the Titans suffer the opposite reaction to what they were doing. Record the results of her spell below.

Case Alert: The energy bursts hide the letters for the first clue in cracking Robin's big case. Remember, a good detective keeps track of all the clues.

Titans	Jinx
Go	s _ _ _ p _
Freeze	_ _ _ m _
Fly	w a l k
Victory	c _ _ _ _ _
Repair	r _ _ _ _ k

1st clue to crack the case:
shadek

Our next mission was full of fireworks when Starfire's big sister, Blackfire, flew in for a surprise visit. It's hard not having your family nearby, and even harder for Starfire, being the only Tamaran female on Earth. I've tried to help her understand our culture, but things can get lost in translation. No matter how confusing life becomes, Starfire knows she can always count on my friendship.

Unfortunately, some unfriendly alien probes paid us a visit at the same time. Funny how Blackfire knew exactly where to aim her starbolts to do the most damage, yet she claimed she'd never seen these probes before. They kept chasing Starfire like she was a criminal on the run and they were the cops. It had to be a case of mistaken identity because Starfire doesn't steal, lie, or keep secrets from her friends.

STARFIRE

Starfire is kind, gentle, innocent, and a very loyal friend. She can recite six thousand verses of a poem about gratitude — and she will. She finds beauty in everything and for some reason loves to drink mustard. She wants to understand others because she cares, even in the middle of battle. She always asks, "Why?" and waits for the answer. This doesn't mean she isn't a fierce fighter. Nobody wants to be on the receiving end of her starbolts. Her emotions power her flight ability and energy blasts. Boundless confidence fuels her strength. Unbridled joy sends her soaring among the clouds. Righteous fury knocks out the criminals. Yet she continues to believe in the best in people. I wish I could, too.

Blackfire is the complete opposite. She has black hair and violet eyes instead of

Blackfire

fiery red hair and green eyes. She flies and hurls purple energy blasts from her hands and also from her eyes. She's older, more experienced, and pretty vocal about it. She tells exciting stories about her many space trips, laughs at Beast Boy's jokes, outplays Cyborg at his favorite video games, writes more depressing poems than Raven, teaches me all the cool, alien martial arts moves, and brought Starfire a rare diamond necklace. Do we like her better than Starfire? No way. For starters, she didn't care when her little sister needed help because it was part of her plan. Once the Centari cops told us what she'd done . . . well, like I said, there were fireworks.

Mistaken Identity

Having stolen the Centari Moon Diamond, Blackfire constantly changed her "look" in the hopes the Centari cops on her trail would arrest Starfire instead of her. Find the "real" Blackfire among the fakes. Catch her before she gets away!

Blackfire claims she flew around a black hole in the Centari system. A black hole is formed when a huge star dies. The heart is called the singularity and its gravitational pull is so strong that nothing — spaceships, planets, nor light itself — can escape.

Alien Translation

Starfire is confused by different meanings for several Earth words. Match her definitions with the correct words from the list below.

Case Alert: The second clue to cracking Robin's big case is among the definitions. Hint: It has nothing to do with food or fun. Remember to keep track of all the clues.

(1) This food comes from the store, not from the garbage can.

(2) Earthlings love these noisy light shows. In my home world, these signaled an enemy attack.

(3) This candy is delicious, but only if it is pink in color.

(4) These are good to eat when they hold ice cream. If they are orange and on the road, they help people drive their cars safely.

(5) These grow in dirt, not in couches.

(6) This can be done with friends, and you do not have to activate a freeze disk.

(7) I do not find these very practical, but Beast Boy practices them on us.

(8) Robin makes these for us to be victorious over the villains.

Cones

Cotton

Chilling

Fireworks

Plans

Potatoes

Junk

Jokes

2nd clue to crack the case:
JUNK

23

Blackfire tried borrowing more than Starfire's clothes. But no one, not even her sister, could ever replace Starfire. I wouldn't let alien cops take her away, so I wasn't about to let her fly off thinking we wouldn't notice if she left. We talked it over. It's good to make new friends, but you don't forget about your old friends. Starfire understands how special she is to us. This team wouldn't be the same without her.

The day Cyborg quit the team proved how necessary each Titan is for our success. A walking block of concrete named Cinderblock staged a jailbreak. Cy and I unleashed our "Sonic Boom" — but ended up immobilizing the team. I know now our timing was off, but back then, all we could do was yell and blame each other.

At least I was right about the mastermind behind this plan. Slade crafted the jailbreak to cover up Cinderblock's real target: freeing Prisoner 385901, a metamorph called Plasmus.

Cinderblock

Huge in body yet tiny in mind, Cinderblock is merely a foot soldier for Slade. But those feet and fists do major damage. He stomped and smashed his way through the prison walls while swatting us like mosquitoes. That's why we needed the "Sonic Boom." Cy's sonic cannon plus my explosive disks pack a strong enough punch to knock out a big guy like Cinderblock. But the timing's got to be just right in order for it to work.

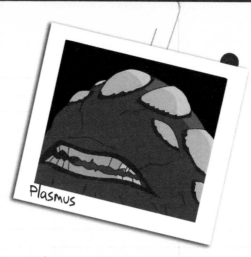
Plasmus

Plasmus is a handful, even after you catch him. His secret human form lives deep beneath his oozing exterior. Otto Von Furth isn't a problem when asleep — that's why the prison kept him in a suspended-animation tank. When he's awake, however, he becomes this gelatinous blob able to hurl awful-tasting goop and spawn creatures made out of sludge. A mouthful of Plasmus tastes worse than a spoonful of Star's Pudding of Sadness!

Police spotted Plasmus guzzling toxic waste at the chemical factory. We planned on popping that giant zit, but couldn't make a lasting dent. Then the call came in about Cinderblock's downtown rampage. With two criminals causing big trouble at opposite ends of town, us down a teammate, and our hands already full . . . we felt the pressure. I thought that by splitting up, we could overwhelm Plasmus, then solve our other problems.

Plasmus had similar ideas: He divided himself into sludge creatures and chased us. The other Titans got slimed while I almost took a bath in a chemical stew. Thankfully, Cyborg's loyalty is bigger than his pride. He loaned me a helping hand in the nick of time.

Cyborg's got the sonic and I've got the boom. Sonic waves coupled with explosive disks knocked Plasmus out cold. Hope he enjoys a long nap.

Cy and I are cool again. He even brought me a gift: Cinderblock, wrapped in steel girders.

BEAST BOY

Whenever the going gets tough, count on Beast Boy for a mood-lifting wise-crack. We also count on his quick, animorphic changes in combat. In a tight spot? A spider crawls through the cracks. Huge bad guy from the Stone Age blocking the way? Pterodactyl assault followed by a T rex stomp eliminates the obstacle. Mad about being the butt of his latest practical joke? Starfire declared him a "klor-bag-varbler-nelk" after his joke hurt her feelings, but she couldn't resist his cute kitty-face and sincere apology.

As annoying as he can be with his bad jokes, Beast Boy values being a good teammate and friend more than a punch line. He learned how important it is to use your gifts wisely and shares his knowledge with those around him. Maybe it's not easy being green, but Beast Boy makes it look like fun.

Lightning

Thunder

We've handled criminals with amazing abilities before, but this time we dealt with forces of nature that came to life.

Thunder and Lightning command the powers of the storm. Their idea of amusement caused havoc on the bridge. Thin as an electrical bolt, Lightning played laser tag with Starfire while his cloud-shaped brother, Thunder, outboomed Cyborg's sonic cannon. When Slade entered the picture, he twisted their warped idea of fun so that they almost destroyed the city. The pair realized their mistake and, by using their powers for good instead of evil, rained out a flame-monster's parade.

Thunder can't exist without lightning. Like a giant spark, lightning can heat the air around it up to thirty thousand degrees Celsius. The heat causes the air to expand, which creates a shock wave. The "boom" is thunder.

While the rest of the Titans focused on cooling off the city, I confronted the "humble old man" who ignited our problems. He greeted me by name. At that moment, I knew *his* name — Slade, the man pulling everyone's strings. A lightning bolt shattered his mask, yet I never saw his true face because he wore another mask beneath it. He vanished in a puff of smoke, leaving behind his insignia and more questions.

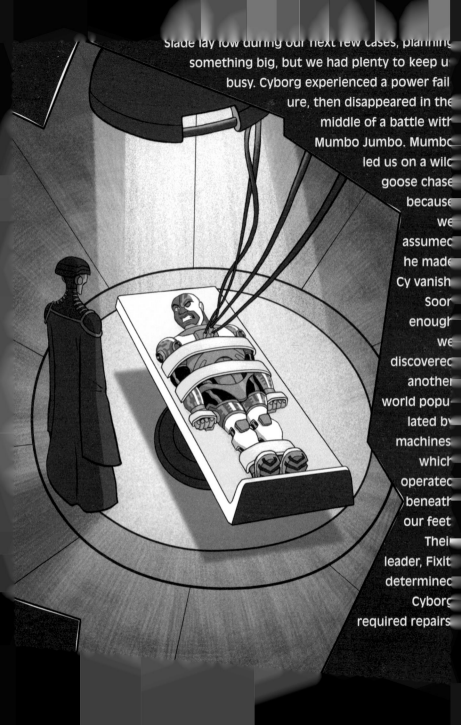

Slade lay low during our next few cases, planning something big, but we had plenty to keep us busy. Cyborg experienced a power failure, then disappeared in the middle of a battle with Mumbo Jumbo. Mumbo led us on a wild goose chase because we assumed he made Cy vanish. Soon enough, we discovered another world populated by machines which operated beneath our feet. Their leader, Fixit, determined Cyborg required repairs.

Assembly Required

Fixit finished his diagnostic analysis of Cyborg: damage is fifty percent and repairs are needed. His plans are listed below in a numeric program language. Cyborg only read part of Fixit's code key: F=6 / I=9 / T=20 / X=24. Now he has to create his own code key to translate Fixit's language and learn his plans.

Case Alert: The first two words are the third clue to cracking Robin's big case. Remember, a good detective keeps track of all the clues.

A	B	C	D	E	F	G	H	I	J	K	L	M
1	2	3	4	5	**6**	7	8	**9**	10	11	12	13
n	**O**	**P**	**Q**	**R**	**S**	**T**	**U**	**V**	**W**	**X**	**Y**	**Z**
14	15	16	17	18	19	**20**	21	22	23	**24**	25	26

FIXIT'S CODED MESSAGE:

TO MAKE CYBORG **100%**
20 15   13 1 11 5   3 25 2 15 18 7

WE MUST REPLACE
23 5   13 21 19 20   18 5 16 12 1 3 5

HIS BIOLOGICAL
8 9 19   2 9 15 12 15 7 9 3 1 12

COMPONENTS
3 15 13 16 15 14 5 14 20 19

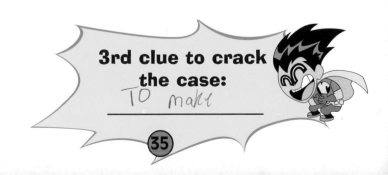

3rd clue to crack the case:
TO MAKE

35

Mumbo Jumbo

Fixit

These two masterminds share nothing in common except we met them and canceled their plans on the same day!

A cybernetic hermit, Fixit leads a community of robotic beings that live underground. He rescued a powerless Cyborg after our friend tumbled through a hole in the junkyard and landed in his kingdom. His dedication to upgrades nearly made him replace those "imperfect" human parts. A memory dump from Cy's system reminded Fixit there is more to life than meets the eye-cam.

Another guy in a cape and mask running around my town meant the hook for Mumbo Jumbo! A former stage magician now employing his skills for theft and mayhem, Mumbo waves his magical wand and recites corny one-liners while robbing the citizens. His colorful scarves and stuffed rabbits thrown from his top hat delayed his capture. I broke his wand and brought down the curtain on his show.

CYBORG

Half-machine and half-man, Cyborg rarely talks about his life before the accident that altered his appearance, but he's still an all-star athlete. No matter what's gone down beforehand — be it an argument or a battery failure — Cy can't warm the bench when the Titans are on the field. If he's not kicking bad-guy butt, you'll find him in the gym maintaining his muscles, in his room tuning up his circuitry and designing awesome all-terrain vehicles, or on the couch playing game station.

Quick with the comebacks and fast on the draw with his sonic cannon, Cyborg is virtually unstoppable. His arms are equipped with diagnostic, defensive, and communication systems; his fingers house minicameras and cutting torches; his viselike mechanical grip bends steel; his enhanced sight records the beauty of a spring day spent with friends. Cy's dedication to the team never crashes. He knows it's the stuff connected to the heart that really matters, not the flashy hardware surrounding it.

Dr. Light

Dressing like a human lightbulb is one thing, but being able to actually manipulate energy made Dr. Light a serious villain in need of an off-switch. Our night fight in the streets lit up the city. The glare made fighting almost impossible, until he taunted Raven. She's scary if she loses control of her emotions. This time, she let her temper take over and gave Dr. Light the most terrifying mind trip of his life. He's still afraid of the dark.

Light travels fast — about 300,000 kilometers per second — and perfectly straight. Light rays can be controlled by blocking (making a shadow), using a mirror (making a reflection), and using a lens (making a refraction).

Raven felt bad about her temper tantrum. I look at it this way: She knows her issues and she works on them. It's her business. Just because she has secrets doesn't mean she can't be a reliable teammate. But Beast Boy is like a dog with a bone, and he kept hounding her with questions until she retreated into her room. Cyborg dragged BB off to apologize and then we didn't see them for hours. While Starfire worried, I kept telling myself everything would be fine as long as they followed the rules: Respect Raven's privacy, try not to interrupt her meditation, and *never* go

Reflections

Wandering around Raven's room, Beast Boy and Cyborg saw a mysterious message. A mirror will reverse the images below, and then everyone can read the message.

Case Alert: Collect the message's highlighted letters, then unscramble the word to learn the fourth clue in cracking Robin's big case. Have you been a good detective and kept track of the clues?

BEWARE
GAZING INTO
RAVEN'S
MIRROR

4th clue to crack
the case:

_R O O M_

RAVEN

A mystical telekinetic, Raven uses her mind to pack a punch. She must finish her mantra of "Azarath, Metrion, Zinthos" before she can unleash her mental energy. Her thoughts heal, create shields, and manipulate inanimate objects. Emotional outbursts unsettle her because, like Starfire, her thoughts and emotions control her powers. Cy and BB learned firsthand that her magical mirror is not a toy, but a personal meditation tool used as a portal into the multidimensional world of her mind.

Since finding peace, quiet, and tranquility for her daily meditation within Titan Tower is almost impossible, Raven fiercely guards her privacy, and she often retreats into her room. She prefers books, sad poems, goth music, dark colors, and being left alone to games, surprises, group hugs, and jokes. Unafraid to speak her mind, she excels at focusing our efforts and possesses a sharp eye for details. Beast Boy calls her "Mystery Girl." It's okay to have secrets as long as they don't interfere with your ability to get the job done.

Puppet King

The next mission turned into a sleepwalking nightmare when the Puppet King sent us a care package we never should have opened.

Apparently once a wooden doll with strings, the Puppet King somehow ended up with a human soul and a deep need to make the world his stage. He crafted these creepy mini-replicas of the Titans and cast a spell, transferring our souls into the puppets while gaining control over our bodies. Raven's counter spell spared her and Starfire the same fate we endured — being on the wrong end of the control stick while this guy pulled our strings.

We thought we had it bad, helpless inside these wooden dummies, only able to watch as the Puppet King ordered our human bodies around like walking zombies and made us attack our friends. Turns out, the girls were dealing with a similar situation — their spirits got switched between their bodies. Raven struggled against unleashing her emotions to activate Starfire's powers, while Star tried to maintain her concentration in order to control Raven's powers. Nobody had control except the Puppet King, and he was up to no good.

Somehow, amid the running and hiding from our drooling counterparts, the girls made time to understand one another better. A little female bonding went a long way because the girls saved our butts. They managed not to beat up our zombie bodies too badly and rescued our wooden ones before the Puppet King torched them. Once Raven — acting through Starfire's body — zapped his magical cauldron, the Puppet King lost all his control, and our spirits returned to their rightful owners.

Although none of us will ever look at a puppet the same way again, one good thing did come out of this freaky experience. Starfire and Raven get along much better now, having walked in each other's shoes.

Aqualad

Heroes answer a call for help wherever there's trouble, be it underground, outer space, or underwater! This mission hurled us out of our depth — six fathoms below the surface — until the "local hero" bailed us out of trouble and we joined forces to catch the bad guy.

The hometown hero of Atlantis, Aqualad breathes underwater and on land, swims at high speeds, and tele-pathically communicates with every sea creature. We crossed paths in the pursuit of the same dangerous criminal. His whale pals towed our damaged T-sub back to his cavern for repairs, while he and Beast Boy con-tinued the underwater hunt. Now the Titans have a teammate "on call" whenever we need special aquatic aid.

Cyborg is our mechanical genius above water, while Tramm is Aqualad's underwater fix-it fish-buddy. Cy thought the T-sub was sunk for good until Tramm

Trident

Tramm

hauled out his treasure chest of tools and they started talking shop.

Tired of being the big fish in a small pond, Trident left Atlantis with a plan: hatch a super-perfect army of clones and take over the world. His environmentally unfriendly theft of forty gallons of toxic waste off a supply ship snagged our attention. Although Slade wasn't involved, I got the feeling these two would have hit it off, unless they got into a competition about who was the baddest.

Scientists believe whales may have been around from fifty-five to sixty million years ago. Today, eighty species of whales live in our oceans, with fossils of these varieties dating back five to seven million years ago.

We activated the T-sub's hydrojet engines and, [u]
s aquatic launch tube, set out to find this amphibious
[ed,] an ambush sent the T-sub into a tailspin!

Once Tram finished his repairs, we zipped back in[to]
[t]he seismic blasters back online, Tram sealed off Trider[t]
[ot.] It's a good thing Trident loves his own company be[cause]
[hi]s clones will be stuck inside that cavern for a long time[.]

Sending Messages

Sea creatures throughout the underwater kingdom received Aqaulad's important message about the Titans' latest mission. To hear his thoughts, read his telephathic waves in a clockwise direction.

Slade's return prompted my decision to fly solo, without clueing in the Titans on my plan. Slade wanted those computer chips. If another criminal stole those items and offered him a partnership, would he trust that individual enough to bring them under his wing?

Red-X blew into town and blew away the Titans. He knew how to defeat each of them: short circuit Cyborg's system, tape shut Raven's mouth, immobilize Starfire's powered-up fists, gum up Beast Boy's ani-morphic quick-change act. And me? Snag me in a net.

I was caught, definitely, but it was a net of my own making. I believed this was the right course of action, the only chance I had to get close enough to gain Slade's trust, learn his identity and intentions, then shut him down permanently. I thought I could fool Slade. I thought I could handle it. I thought the Titans would understand. We do whatever's necessary to stop the bad guys . . . right?

Wrong on every count, starting with the biggest mistake I made — hiding the truth from my team. I betrayed their friendship. When I pulled off Red-X's mask and they saw my face staring out at them, I also saw their faces fill with shock and disappointment. If I didn't trust my team, then how could they trust me? Slade was right on the mark when he said, "Trust took me to build, yet was so easy to break."

Slade

Who is the man behind the mask? Where is his headquarters? Why is this criminal mastermind dispatching a slew of supervillains and android ninjas to destroy the Teen Titans instead of coming after us himself? The deeper I dug into the mystery of Slade, the more questions I unearthed.

He's skilled in several martial arts, including the bo staff. His armor hints at a military background. His mask exposes one eye, so is the other injured? He's patient, moving his pieces carefully on the chessboard. He's resourceful, probably independently wealthy. He hired a score of agents to do his dirty work. Cinderblock is locked up. Plasmus slumbers in his deprivation chamber. The H.I.V.E. agents serve detention. Thunder and Lightning's evil ways evaporated. We're onto Slade. Who could he possibly send after us? Finally, he'll have to take us on, mano a mano!

ROBIN

It's fitting I write my own profile opposite the profile of my archenemy. Slade pushes me to be better, smarter, faster. I don't have superpowers. I depend on my intellect, courage, acrobatic skills, martial-arts training, and a gadget-packed Utility Belt. My cape is made of high-density polymerized titanium, ten times stronger than steel. I can't fly on my own. I store cutting torches and lock picks in my gloves, not in my fingers like Cyborg. My belt is loaded with tools: multipurpose throwing disks able to freeze, explode, and electronically disrupt; bolos; a collapsible bo staff, which extends from either end; Birdarangs with cable attachments; and the Titan locator and com unit.

Although I am dedicated to training, I take time out to be with my friends. I love beating Cy and BB at video games, explaining different Earth customs to Starfire, and making sure Raven has some fun. I used to be a sidekick, the protégé of an incredible mentor. Now I'm the leader of an amazing team. Yet . . . sometimes I wonder if Slade is trying to teach me lessons about myself that I really don't want to learn.

RED X

On the rooftop, I gave everything I had in a brawl with Slade. I left my bo staff hooked on my Utility Belt. I used fists and wit, but it wasn't enough. He caught my cape and threw me the length of the rooftop. I smashed into a stack of crates, slipped, and lost my balance. But instead of falling, Slade saved me. He wasn't through with me, yet. His plans had only begun. I knocked him out . . . or thought I did.

Instead, "Slade" was an android, and the real Slade talked with me via remote, promising a future showdown.

Slade figured me out, yet I still don't know his identity
his plans. As much as I hate to admit it, Slade and I are alike. We
focused, serious, determined, and hate to lose. But he does
have anyone he can trust, while I have four incredible friends
Cyborg, Beast Boy, Raven, and Starfire — who I can always cou
on.

I better go apologize to them again and promise that
matter what happens, the Teen Titans will stick together. Victory
sweeter when you can share it with your friends.

Titanic Terms

Hold on, it's not over yet! There are a lot of terms to know if you're a Teen Titan. Search for the words listed below within the grid on the opposite page. Look forward, backward, diagonally, and even upside down!

Case Alert: The leftover letters in the puzzle form the final clue in cracking Robin's big case. Have you been a good detective and kept all the clues? Put the pieces together to find out Slade's sinister plan.

Terms to Find

agents

aliens

android

animal

Atlantis

battle

betrayal

birdarang

bo staff

criminal

fly

friend

gear

go

headquarters

his

illusion

karate

lair

machine

masks

meditate

ninja

pizza

power up

share

skills

sonic

steal

starbolts

sub

team

tower

trust

truth

unite

utility belt

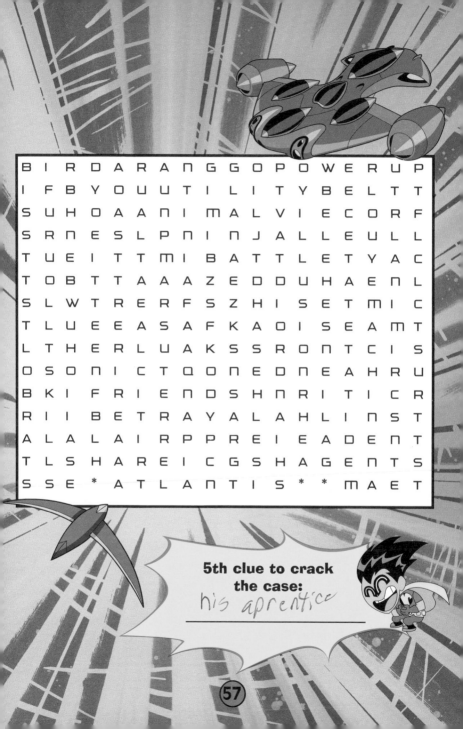

```
B I R D A R A N G G O P O W E R U P
I F B Y O U U T I L I T Y B E L T T
S U H O A A N I M A L V I E C O R F
S R N E S L P N I N J A L L E U L L
T U E I T T M I B A T T L E T Y A C
T O B T T A A A Z E D D U H A E N L
S L W T R E R F S Z H I S E T M I C
T L U E E A S A F K A O I S E A M T
L T H E R L U A K S S R O N T C I S
O S O N I C T Q O N E D N E A H R U
B K I F R I E N D S H N R I T I C R
R I I B E T R A Y A L A H L I N S T
A L A L A I R P P R E I E A D E N T
T L S H A R E I C G S H A G E N T S
S S E * A T L A N T I S * * M A E T
```

**5th clue to crack
the case:**

his aprentice

57

ANSWER KEY

Page 9: The TV's remote control is on the coffee table.

Page 14: "Cyborg's Walking Tour"

Page 16: "Opposite Reaction"

TITANS	JINX
Go	**S**top
Freeze	Me**l**t
Fly	F**a**ll
Victory	**D**efeat
Repair	Br**e**ak

1st clue to crack the case: **SLADE**

Page 22: "Mistaken Identity"

Page 23: "Alien Translation"

Definitions
(1) Junk
(2) Fireworks

(3) Cotton
(4) Cones
(5) Potatoes
(6) Chilling
(7) Jokes
(8) Plans

2nd clue to crack the case: **PLANS**

Page 35: "Assembly Required"

A	B	C	D	E	F	G	H	I	J	K	L	M
1	2	3	4	5	6	7	8	9	10	11	12	13

N	O	P	Q	R	S	T	U	V	W	X	Y	Z
14	15	16	17	18	19	20	21	22	23	24	25	26

Fixit's coded message:
TO MAKE CYBORG 100% WE MUST REPLACE
HIS BIOLOGICAL COMPONENTS

3rd clue to crack the case: **TO MAKE**

Page 40: "Reflections"
BEWARE GAZING INTO RAVEN'S MIRROR

4th clue to crack the case: **ROBIN**

Page 49: "Sending Messages"

Aqualad's telepathic message to his fish buddies:

KEEP TRIDENT AND HIS CLONES SEALED INSIDE HIS LAIR.

Pages 56-57: "Titanic Terms"

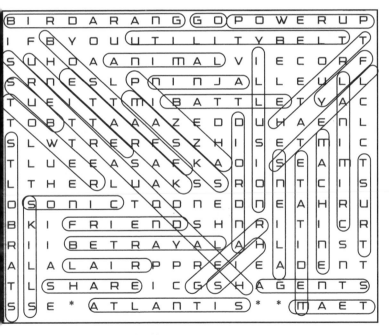

5th clue to crack the case:

IF YOU HAVE COLLECTED ALL THE CLUES THE LAST

ONE IS **HIS APPRENTICE**

Did you crack the case?
The answer was in pieces hidden throughout the book.

The question is:
What is Slade planning?
The answer is:
Slade plans to make Robin his apprentice.